INTO THE
STORYVERSE

To Andrew
Welcome to the
Storyverse -
Best wishes

George
30·7·2020

GEORGE JOHNSTON

Into the Storyverse
© George Johnston 2020

ISBN: 978-1-922340-92-4 (Paperback)
         978-1-922340-93-1 (eBook)

 A catalogue record for this book is available from the National Library of Australia

Lead Editor: Kristy Martin
Editors: Beverley Streater and Marisa Parker
Cover Design: Ocean Reeve Publishing
Original Cover Image: Victoria Fitzpatrick
Design and Typeset: Ocean Reeve Publishing
Printed in Australia by Ocean Reeve Publishing

Published by George Johnston and Ocean Reeve Publishing
www.oceanreevepublishing.com

REEVE
PUBLISHING

Preface

So, you have this book in your hand. A whole spectrum of possibility lies before you. Yes, it is constrained by language and bound by paper, but you are holding something fundamental to life: a story. Stories connect us and enrich lives. Stories tap into something we all have: imagination. I envisage you assessing the value of this book. Maybe you are thinking, *What's* Into the Storyverse *about? What will I be getting into if I delve into this tale?* Let me explain.

The *Storyverse* is the universe of connected stories that surround us. It is a world as evocative and as real as the one you currently inhabit. How can it be real if it is fiction? Simple, you read the words and as your imagination takes flight, the story becomes tangible to you. Every moment of every day you live out a story that is yours alone. The sad fact is many people have grafted someone else's fiction onto their own special story. They have listened to fears induced by themselves and others and have sunk into anxiety and depression. Struggle is fundamental to life and it is infused into the fabric of this story told through traditional narrative and poetic verse. It is innovative and unique and I hope you can set your imagination free and enter *Into the Storyverse*.

The main character is about to walk out of the next page and into your imagination. His name is Dusty. You will follow him; looking over his shoulder and inside his

1

head. He lives in South East Queensland, his parents hailed from South East Asia, but he is most at home on the road traveling to where his heart takes him.

Dusty's journey is one of faith, but the language in his head is not the language he speaks because words are, and always will be, inadequate; getting twisted and convoluted with use. Actions speak louder than words. For Dusty, the creative force that holds everything together is love. He names this 'God'. But Dusty has no appetite for academic discussions about belief. His world is shaped by his experience of grief and loss. You are about to enter into this world and while words can never be enough, they can be evocative. As you read, disconnect yourself from where ever you are physically and open your mind to the Storyverse. Enough preamble, it's time to turn the page. Dusty is about to walk across the aftermath of a devastating bushfire.

Tall choking walls of smoke turned day into night then flames brought a hell on earth that was halted only by the ocean. That was yesterday, a day burned into his memory. He is crossing this black no-man's-land from the narrow sanctuary of the Tasmanian beach. Only ashes and charred memories of life remain here. He absently touches his arms and face, feeling the scars that were seared into his skin years before yesterday's violent conflagration.

In the smoking silence, there is only the feeble intrusion of his boots crunching on the gravel and the rasping of each laboured breath as his lungs struggle with the polluted air. Stooping to place his hands on his bent knees, his head dips as if the weight of maintaining life is crushing down on him. In this position, the straps of his backpack pull awkwardly on his neck and shoulders. He had forgotten about the burden for just a moment. The contents of his pack call to him again, pulling him back to a reality that he is not ready to face.

It is now exactly one month since his closest friend Alan died by his own hand, leaving Dusty with only ashes and some artefacts to carry with him. As he sinks to his knees, a casual observer may assume that he is in prayer or overwhelmed by the destruction that lies before him. The reality is more complicated. The horror of yesterday's destruction merely sparks his memory of being close to death and feeling powerless to protect the people around him. Dusty had not been able to accept any hugs of consolation after Alan's suicide, for in his heart he strongly felt that he was responsible for his friend's death. It all started for him years ago in an overturned car at the bottom of a gully. If only he had known what to do at that time, then maybe things would have ended differently. For Alan, it all started even further back in time.

Turning back to the sea, he reaches the gritty sand and sheds his clothes like a snake awkwardly shrugging off its skin. The ocean, with its rolling surf, draws him into its embrace.

Floating free
In the foaming sea
I dip between each cresting wave
I look ahead and I am almost brave
As water rears up then curves down
To the sandy hidden ground
Will the wave smash me
Or can I ride it free?
Either way, it's up to me
Floating in the moment
Between the bad that was
And the good that can be
Or was that the good that was
And the bad that can be?
Either way, there is not much time
Duck under the wave
Or ride it in
Maybe it's better
To avoid looking at what was
Or what might be
Just stay in the current
Floating free.

As he steps out of the water, the embrace of the sea breeze cools Dusty's back and his body shivers. Scooping up his towel, he dries the salty moisture with vigorous urgency. The rough comfort of the towel is tempered by his old friend, Regret, which smothers him with another unwelcome hug. He shrugs off Regret's advances, but some feelings are hard to fully shake. They hang on like the smoky odour that now taints his clothes. He dresses, transferring coarse sand from clothing to skin. The discomfort this brings is nothing compared to what he feels when he looks at his backpack.

The backpack he had earlier cast aside in his haste to reach the sea lies in a sand crater like an unexploded bomb. It is his load to carry; his burden to bear. In its zipped-up depths are four items he needs to deal with, but he is not ready to do so. Rather than bring the items out into the open, he instead lifts his gaze and surveys the ruins of the town. The forest that had once sheltered the community, fed the fire that destroyed it. The very thing that had provided comfort and beauty to the townsfolk turned on them. And this all happened in a day. At least no one had died.

Just a week ago, Dusty had been poring over a map of this area, imagining what it would be like to explore the numerous tracks that snaked into the hills. He loved maps, and he loved filling in maps in his mind, then testing what he saw on paper against what he discovered when he got there.

I like maps, the world laid out on paper
Because they capture something … something good
A map shows what's out there but what I see
Is never everything, there is always something new
Maps define the boundaries of our world
Imagination plays with what might be there
Experience fills the gaps
But that's not the end
Everything exists in relationship with something else
Nothing stays the same forever
Maps are a starting point laid out on paper
Dream, explore, discover
But don't be fooled into thinking
That there is nothing new to discover
Maps define space but we move through time
With the one who is—yesterday, today, forever
I look at a map and the map's symbols capture my
imagination
Then I go on a journey in which I
Hold captive the thoughts that are not helpful to me
And I see what's really out there
On that unique day
Then with words, I hope to
Capture something
Something good.

The flames did not respect the boundaries printed on Dusty's map. Reality was like that; it had a way of burning through expectation. He had come to this place assuming he would find a peaceful sanctuary, quarantined from reminders of Alan that were infused into the fabric of his hometown of Brisbane. That was two weeks ago before the fire had introduced yet another sudden transformation in his life.

He views the blackened hills that had once been so green and full of life, and his gaze drops to the map, following the contour lines that swirl like complex finger-prints around the town. A single fat tear stains the map, followed by another. He rubs his eyes and tilts his face up, feeling the sky weep as if it too mourns the loss of the green land. He does not seek shelter as the drizzle turns to rain, but he does carefully fold the map and place it back in the depths of his pack, purposely avoiding the collection of items that lie entombed in the base of his bag.

As much as Dusty tries to capture unhelpful thoughts, sometimes they capture him. At this moment he is seized by grief as his fingers brush the contents of his bag. There is a knife, an antique fob watch, a small urn containing Alan's ashes, and a sealed tin. He retracts his hand, trying to sever the connections between grief and guilt that coil their way up his hand to his heart and mind. Alan has left him with a task to perform and this task will take him to the other side of the world.

Dusty, now in his fourth decade, has always been a man on the move, walking away from his past, recoiling from the future, then standing precariously in the shaky sanctuary of his imagination. He likes to imagine a better world; he longs to make it a better world. If only he had a map to guide him through what lay ahead.

Above him, the stars begin to come out as the world turns to hide from the light again. How did people manage when they had no maps to guide them?

Eternity lit the way
As they crossed the ocean's swell
At the break of day
What stories did they tell?
From the night of stars
Sprinkled on the eternal canvas
Stretched across the ocean's black
Terrors of the deep beneath
And above …
Eternity lighting the way
Black fades into blue, night into day
Though the night was dark
Eternity lit the way
The heavens declare the glory of God …
Who sprinkled stars on a map
An eternal canvas
Lighting our way through
Eternal night, eternal day.

Having slept on the beach, a tiny crab tickle-steps across Dusty's scarred arms, rousing him to full consciousness in the predawn darkness. Orion, Taurus, and the Pleiades are in the sky, as familiar and reliable as ever. He gathers his thoughts together as he gathers his belongings together, feeling his way. But when the sun finally bursts over the horizon, he has once again removed all the items from his bag.

Lifting the knife by its blood-red handle, the surgically sharp blade flashes sunlight in his eyes. He blinks and lifts the gold fob watch, hanging it up by its intricate chain. It spins on its chain and, like the knife, the low sun glints off the back of the watch. As its revolutions slow down, the light flickers like a faulty lighthouse that can no longer warn of danger.

Next, he removes the small urn and runs his fingers over the raised pattern of leaves and flowers adorning the vessel. A random drift of cinder from the bushfire settles on the urn. He brushes it away, only to leave a smear of ash dulling the surface. *Why do my efforts to make things better always make things worse?* This thought lingers longer than it should.

His attention veers to the small, sealed tin. He could open it now but abstains, hanging on to the mystery and its slender thread of hope that some remnant of goodness lies within. He is desperate for some good right now; some encouragement that today will be a better day. After another hour, Dusty rises and heads off away from the beach into the bush. He has a long journey ahead, so he settles into a rhythm of walking.

One foot after another
I walk through the bush
The track rises and falls
It is littered with rocks
Every step is a careful transfer of weight
Every step is a fall arrested as I move
In rhythm with the land
In step with its requirements
It requires my time
It requires my patience
My effort placed into
Placing one foot after the other
The journey is the destination
The destination is not the end
The track I follow is the way
Of truth and life
I follow the way, the truth, the life
One foot after the other
Every step a careful transfer of weight
From sole to soul
One foot after another.

One step at a time; he takes one tentative step at a time. Dusty's future is uncharted territory; one that he desires and fears. He arrives back home in Brisbane where his old Queenslander house lacks the love and attention he is able to give due to his absences from travelling. Home is where the heart is, but his heart is always out searching for another new place to explore. The house is cluttered with souvenirs; shuttered up in cupboards, sealed off from the light of present-day recollection. Floorboards protest underfoot as he pads down the hallway. In the dark, his hand absently slides along the wall, like a blind man on a Braille trail. He really must replace that light bulb. Entering his bedroom, the suit he wore to Alan's funeral still lays discarded on the bed. If the bedroom was a crime scene, then his suit would be the victim, waiting for forensic examination.

Dusty learned many new and shocking things about his friend on the day of the funeral. Alan's sister, Emily, had spoken to him at length on that day and what she revealed had changed his perception of Alan. Dusty had one last task to perform for him; a task in need of planning, and he was just not ready to tackle what was required.

Though there was much speculation, many of Alan's friends were uncertain why he chose to die by suicide. Yet Dusty, on the outside looking in, was aware of several contributing factors that may have led Alan to take the action that he did. He had been abused as a young boy by a member of the clergy, was the son of alcoholic parents, and had survived a terrible accident that had left him with chronic pain and reduced mobility due to his injuries. Ultimately, Alan's true motivation for his final act would remain a mystery.

After the car accident, Alan had become a recluse. Inspired by the work of Ernst Barlich, the German sculptor who carved many evocative wooden figures during the tumultuous years of World War I, he took up woodcarving. This made little sense to Dusty at the time, but, as a friend, he recognised Alan's talent in carving out miniature human figures, so he bought him a special whittling knife. Alan had great creativity with this tool, but it had been this knife that ended his life. Maybe creativity was like love when it had nowhere to go; a double-edged blade that could cut both ways.

Right now, in a house full of memories, Dusty feels suffocated so he goes outside. In the late afternoon, he takes the Deagon deviation to the southern end of the long bridge to Redcliffe. On impulse, he traverses the mudflats and climbs a mangrove tree.

The mangrove tree has a tangle of branches
A tangle of roots spread into the mud
A chaos of life, a disordered mess that just
Works together to anchor life in one place.
The bridge is linear, ordered
It crosses the space and disappears
In a vanishing point, beyond the mud
An anchor line between home and work.
To travel from one place to another
And miss the tangle of life
That hides in plain sight
Is to travel on a bridge to nowhere.
As you struggle to reach your destination
As you sink into despair
Life is not on the horizon
You are already there.

The glare from the setting sun prevents him from looking to the west where the solar furnace burns across the hills on the skyline. Averting his eyes, he notices the short, spiked mangrove roots jutting up like gnarly fingers casting long shadows. The tree flexes as he moves around to get a better view. This wood is alive, but its real life and mystery lay hidden within.

Alan had often searched for just the right kind of wood to use for his carvings. The texture needed to have a tight, even grain. Alan could bring life to what others considered to be just deadwood, by meticulously shaving it away. But to do this he needed to find the right piece. As his mobility reduced over the years, he came to rely on Dusty to source this wood for him.

Dusty had obtained the wood from privet trees, boxwood from France, limewood, and a range of desert hardwoods. He had hoped to gain some timber from the Tasmanian town that had been erased off the map from the fire, but it was too late for that now. As he had walked through the burnt bush on that morning, he had the bizarre thought that he could have salvaged some of the blackened stumps for Alan to use. He had the crazy idea that he could just remove the black carbon like he was scraping off burnt toast; maybe life could still be carved out of the deadwood? But of course, by that time Alan was gone, and Dusty had no skill with a knife.

He had admired Alan's carvings, but he had also worried that Alan seemed to be locking himself away from the world, isolated in his refuge long into the night.

Everything had its place in Alan's workshop. It was like his small manageable universe. When Dusty had bought Alan the knife, he hadn't realised that Alan needed a range of specialist tools. It was only when he entered his workshop that he realised the full complexity of Alan's craft.

He clambers down the mangrove tree's abrasive bark, tiptoeing his way across the tree roots, trying to plot a course that does not damage them. Had he even thought about that as he hurriedly clomped his way across the mud to climb the tree earlier? Life could be resilient and fragile at the same time, so he places his feet with care. If only he'd been able to step gently and listen clearly on that evening ten years ago when Alan had revealed that he'd been abused by a senior member of the clergy. Dusty's bland words of consolation had trampled on the little tree roots of hope that must have been sprouting in Alan at that time. Dusty's listening skills—like his driving ability—were not helped by them both getting drunk.

He reaches the solid ground of the car park and has a moment of disorientation when time shifts back to the evening that held disastrous consequences for both of them. No, that was then, this is now. He swats the memory away. Squinting into the sun, he walks towards his car with his long shadow trailing behind him.

Shadow man on the wall
On the ground trailing behind me
Elongated, distorted, memories tainted
By guilt, regret, sadness, but always
Behind me as I walk toward the light
Of a better day dawning
The sharp knife of each moment
Cuts between the past and the future
We only have a moment … then another … and another
On and on, as the shadow man on the wall, trailing behind
Keeps me humble, grounded, centred, balanced
The lessons of the past and the hope for the future
Distilled into the moment that matters …
This moment
The sacred now.

Some people had told Dusty that their places were more sacred than other places. No, the word they used was 'sanctified'. They built big churches, and then tried to fit a little God in between the walls. You were only to meet this God inside their pretty buildings. It was within the walls of one of those structures that Alan had met his abuser. Afterwards, he'd locked this experience in a deep cellar where no light could touch it. When he had revealed his experience to Dusty—

A truck blew its horn, shattering Dusty back from his thoughts. He moved his car forward through the traffic lights which he realised had been green for some time. Accelerating up to speed, it was as if the traffic around him was urging him to travel faster. In a way, he just wanted to slow down to plot a new course, but some highways funnelled you to where they wanted to take you. In the life they had before the accident, Dusty and Alan had spent a lot of time off the beaten track, exploring many remote mountains.

The terrible irony was that when Alan had revealed his full history of abuse to Dusty, he no longer saw himself as a victim but a survivor who was learning how to thrive. In a foolish moment of carelessness, Dusty had lost control of the car and had erased Alan's capacity to reach those mountain tops. They had ended up at the bottom of a steep gully in a tangle of twisted metal and crushed dreams.

Dusty applies a little more pressure on the brake to lose the tailgater. He has no desire to have another accident. Glancing up for a moment, he notices a pair of gliding pelicans tracking a lazy path across the sky. The brief sight of the pelicans instantly transports Dusty back to a cold harbor in Tasmania years before Alan's suicide. Recalling the memory, the surge of confident idealism he felt then feels foreign to him now.

Surfing the wind
Wings extended
Dive down
Soar up
Curve around
Call out
Birds mastering the flow of air
The air we breathe
That keeps us alive
Our eyes water in the icy wind
The breath of life
That keeps us alive
The old man watching the birds said,
'You know you're alive when you feel
the cold wind numb your face.'
I thought this was a dumb statement
Then I saw the birds surfing the wind
And then I saw more
Extending my arms like a bird
I accepted the life God breathed into me
Surfing the wind
That blows the dust out of my mind
Right out of my core
I am grounded
And yet I soar.

That day by the harbour seemed so long ago now. He realises that he is clutching the steering wheel tightly. He loosens his grip and scans the road ahead. The traffic is becoming more congested and slowing down.

Dusty and Alan had been good mates for years. They were both writers. They were both people of faith. But they both stayed away from the formal church for different reasons. For Alan, that reason was obvious if you knew his story. For Dusty, it was a different story. He could see life in people but found it harder when those people circled the wagons and formed a club. Clubs had rules that defined who was in and who was out.

He reaches a large roundabout close to his home. In the dying light, a ring of red brake lights encircles the large mound of grass that has been claimed by two plovers. Their custard yellow faces look out at the traffic with puritanical indignation. They swoop ineffectively at passing cyclists with a ridiculous 'ack ack ack ack' sound.

Dusty taps the steering wheel impatiently. Peering ahead he sees the road blocked by an overturned car. As the traffic inches forward everyone turns to look at the accident. *What is this fascination with staring dumbly at other people's misfortune?* He wonders if the fascination is linked to relief that it has happened to someone else. Maybe it is also linked to the suppressed idea one day it could be them getting cut out of a vehicle.

Dusty recalls a carved Christ hanging on a church wall. The face had so much pain etched into it. He hated seeing pain in others because he felt it as his own, even though he could never fully understand it. Alan had been able to give expressions to the faces that he carved out of wood; expressions of pain or delight. It amazed Dusty how carving to make the surface uneven, gave definitions that animated the wood. It was something about how the light cast shadows on the faces. In the art of carving, shadow was colour.

Night has fallen. Dusty weeps in the dark seclusion of his car. A part of him feels like driving on and on, just for the sake of doing something. Doing nothing does not seem like a good option.

In my darkest moments
When fear pushes
A relentless, pressing weight down
The depressing wait time
I am waiting for solutions
I feel like a child in pain
And I turn to you like a child in pain
And you remind me whose child I am
This exercise of faith, of trust
Takes me to some ugly, raw places
Where I don't want to go
Sometimes it feels like there is nothing that I wouldn't do
To avoid the struggle
But without the struggle
I would probably do nothing.

He turns into the driveway of his old Queenslander. Opening the front door, he breathes in the familiar musty smell of a house that has been shut up in the heat for too long. He walks through the empty home, opening windows to let in the evening air that brings with it the hum of cars and buses moving slowly along the busy road. He crashes onto his bed and is lost to the world for the next seven hours.

The next morning, after eating a cooked breakfast then washing the dishes, he sits at the kitchen bench with the morning light flooding the room. He still wears the pink rubber gloves he must use to stop the detergent affecting his dermatitis. The cutlery is laid out on a tea towel. With one hand holding a handkerchief over his nose to ward off a sneeze, he looks like a surgeon preparing to operate, and in a way he is. He has placed the knife from his backpack on the table and is aiming to dissect, maybe even excise, his guilt. Not physically but merely poking at it, performing a spiritual biopsy.

The whittling knife is lifted to the light and Dusty studies the long blade that is scalpel-sharp. He had given this very knife to Alan as a gift. Alan's talent had fashioned many little animal figures out of wood which he had given to Dusty. These cute creatures, that with the passage of time had become a mute accusatory menagerie, now sit in regimented rows on wall shelves staring at Dusty with dead eyes.

He had gifted Alan the knife. Alan had used the knife to take his own life. This fact causes Dusty to feel burning shame as if he was the one who had done the killing.

He rises to the kitchen window noticing the quiet of the morning is replaced with the drone of today's traffic. If this sound is like the heartbeat of the city, then the view of the road is like one of its congested arteries. It is at this moment that he becomes distracted by the sight of a woman walking by the busy road. Her story is known to everyone in the area.

She pushes the pram, her child sleeps, head tilted awkwardly
The weight of his exuberant lust for life has worn him out
She dreams for her child
As the pram wheels crunch stony furrows on the ground
As they walk beside the wide highway, she dreams for her little man
That he may grow and find his place on this long highway of dreams
Lifting her eyes, she sees the traffic as if for the first time this morning
Car wheels turn slowly on the ground;
The drivers crane their heads looking for
A way forward, their heads tilted awkwardly away from the
rising sun
She wonders if this human race is worth winning
She wipes a tear from her bruised face to try to wash away
The memory of her last beating
Her head tilts awkwardly, downward in shame
But she sees her child, her little man, and finds hope on this day
Wheels might turn slowly, grinding furrows on the ground
But as People of the Way, there is always something lost
And something new to be found.

She disappears into the distance. All his neighbours think they know her story, but Dusty has never seen them chatting with her. Maybe they have just made up her story to suit their own need for idle talk. Gossip feeds off a desire that is not healthy, usually a desire to denigrate someone. Dusty wonders what compels the woman to travel that hard road every day. Maybe like everyone else, she just takes one step at a time. If all the world's a stage and we are all merely actors, then Dusty is determined not to play any role assigned to him. He sits on his front step a while watching the regular cast of characters that inhabit his neighbourhood.

The man dressed in office wear stands on an electric scooter scanning the sky as he zips down the footpath. His helmet is crowned with cable ties and his brow is furrowed with concentration as he considers the risks of a magpie attack. School students reluctantly drift down the road to their fate. They part to let crazy Bob shuffle past them, his wild eyes embedded in an explosion of hair that radiates out in all directions. Most people look anywhere but into his eyes. 'Don't look into them' is the unwritten rule. Dusty wonders what lies behind those eyes. Like everyone else, Dusty lowers his eyes when crazy Bob walks past.

Alan's knife rests in Dusty's grip. He is holding Alan's knife. He has been holding on to it for too long now. It is time to leave it behind. He places the knife in a small padded envelope then absurdly wraps it in bubble wrap, then more brown paper. It is as if he means to completely hide it from sight to make it easier to throw away. Maybe he doesn't want anyone else to find it and use it. He walks out of the garden and down the street to the row of shops. In the side road, there are big industrial bins that always seem to be full. He lifts a heavy creaking metal lid and dumps the knife into its shadowy depths.

Reason tells him that he is not directly responsible for Alan's death, but the ache in his heart makes him feel like it is his fault. With the knife lost to the putrid abyss of the bin, Dusty longs to leave behind the stinking feelings of guilt that have been following him around like a bad smell for so long. If only discarding his guilt could be as simple as dumping something into a bin. Life is never that straight forward.

It's never straight forward
This road that winds
It curves up valleys
And rolls down mountains
A ribbon unravelled
To roll down to the sea
I see as far as
The next bend
The next twist of
Fate or chance
Or design
Make straight the path
Make it easy
But no
I am drawn
To see what's around
The corner
The road unravels
And I unravel
With it
In it
I move
And find
The spark
That drives me forward
But it is never straight forward.

He is walking back from the bin looking down at the ground. The concrete path is ruptured by tree roots that over time have made the ground into a fissured obstacle course. Now he knows why the scooter man rides on the other side of the road. Leaf litter lies where it has fallen from trees, in a mixture of natural and unnatural detritus. His gaze follows the spiralling doomed flight of a plastic bag as it lifts in the wind wash from a passing truck, and his attention is drawn to what remains of the bush that still clings to the hillside.

The green hill has been scarred by bulldozers; a shaved strip runs up to the skyline. Old wooden poles linked by badly maintained power lines puncture this wound and the dark wires look like old sutures on a forgotten injury. Red volcanic soil now bleeds off this gash on the landscape.

A tingle on Dusty's back grows stronger with each step that distances him from the bin as if the spectre of the Alan that he thought he knew is following him. Struggling to suppress this irrational thought he almost bumps into crazy Bob and his five energetic Jack Russell terriers. Their eyes meet and Dusty is exposed to a disjointed rant that is directed at anyone nearby. People call him 'crazy Bob' and avoid him like the plague, but as Dusty listens, he hears nothing threatening in Bob's speech.

'I am a very stable genius like that man in the white house but with better hair and teeth and my dogs are well fed and happy and they have good teeth and they wouldn't bite you because I feed them all the good stuff with no chemicals from the government.'

Bob's stories stretch credibility as they are woven in a free-form narrative that constantly threatens to spin off in odd directions. Dusty finds it best to not focus on the accuracy of Bob's tales but more on why they are important to him. Bob's reasoning is odd but he is motivated by his love for his dogs and they do seem to be healthy and happy.

When Dusty leaves Bob to his tangle of dog leashes, he is still confused about the stories but he has understood at least a little bit about what makes him tick: he loves animals. Life is so full of contradiction. Bob probably is crazy, but in his own way he is happy, and for the most part harmless. Dusty passes a house that has a sign in the garden encouraging people to plant more trees to give koalas a habitat to live in. He finds the sign ironic because it is on land that was cleared to make way for the inexorable urban sprawl. The way we all collectively destroy the environment to maintain our lifestyle was to Dusty a kind of socially acceptable craziness.

Alan had seemed to have it all together, but he was gone. The lady with the child has endured so much yet she keeps travelling down that road. Everyone avoids Bob but he is harmless. Dusty can see how easy it is to place labels on other people. Maybe he has done that to himself: Dusty, the guilty party. He has had enough of that. Everyone makes mistakes. No one is perfect. The thought that is teasing its way into his head is simple: *Who I am is enough.*

I am loved
God is love
Love is God
Who I am
Is enough
Love lives inside
Spins me like
A coin spins
With two sides

Image of God
And flawed likeness
Of Love
Living with love
I will fail
I will succeed
But loved I ...
Am loved
God is love
Love is God

Who I am
Is enough.

W ith this simple theology in his head, Dusty walks home. Words are hollow things that either echo in someone's mind or resonate powerfully if the person operates on a similar frequency. He does not want to let his words get ahead of his actions.

The rusty gate to his overgrown garden protests and only reluctantly gives him access. He does not stop to pull out any weeds. Maybe there is a good plant growing in the dark undergrowth waiting to burst into flower one day.

In the past, he had been a proficient gardener, planting flowers in neat rows that added colour for a season. But it took a lot of work. It took a lot of time separating the good plants from the bad ones. And the bad ones always came back. Life in the natural world existed in a tangled profusion that resisted all efforts to impose order on it.

Dusty had met many people who lived to impose order on others. Their life purpose was to show other people the right way to live. They spoke of God and love but were often motivated by fear. He could hear it in what they said; even see it in their faces.

A sudden noise startles him and he looks up to see a possum clattering over the corrugated roof of his house. Just beyond this, the man in the moon has—as always—that perpetual look of surprise. The possum looks back at Dusty and while no words can be spoken, there is more life in that small moment than the many hollow words he has heard from hollow people.

We are wired to look for the face of love
Look up into the sky and see the face of the moon
It is impossible not to see a face on the moon
Because as a child we are wired to see faces
To look up for comfort, reassurance, love
Does the child have someone to look up to?
Or does someone look down on them
With the dead face of the moon?
The face of love has a smile or at least
It is open to remembering that we all began
As a child looking for the reassuring face of love
We are all wired to look for the face of God
In life, in the middle of life
Not just at our beginning and our end.

He reaches the veranda, stepping over a garden tool graveyard that surrounds his tattered welcome mat. The fragrance of his neighbour's white gardenia hangs heavy in the humid air. The garden gate that had been so reluctant to move now slowly screeches open as if wilfully taunting him. He sighs. This is not a new occurrence. Walking back to close the gate, he notices that the woman with the pram is returning down the road.

She stops and crouches in front of her agitated child. For a moment the light catches her face at just the right angle. Dusty can't hear what she says but her body language speaks volumes. He can clearly see the love that she has for her child. It is written in her face. What he does not see is where she has come from, where she has been in life. People could make assumptions about her based on what they think they know of her, but there would always be more they don't understand. Only she knows and understands her own story; it is never far from her recollection. It includes a loss that now drives her to appreciate everything more sharply.

The child is soothed or at least a little more settled, they move on.

Summer's calendar
The white gardenias
Soft petals fall
Marking the season
When life flowered
Perfect, hidden, fleeting
Your tiny heart stopped beating
How I longed for our first meeting
How I longed for your first greeting
Not for me … not to be
You left … before you arrived
Leaving me to wilt like the white gardenia
Summer's calendar marking
My season of guilt
I marked the days, I marked the season
Till when you were due
Was it my fault? Was it me that sinned?
I could find no reason
It was like chasing the wind
That blows upon the white gardenia
Bringing rain and life with such ease
Then scattering petals in the breeze
The wind blows the sad, sweet fragrance in my mind
For summer's calendar now lies discarded
The wind turns cold as days unwind
A season of guilt becomes a season of grief
Each day blows away like a wind-tossed leaf
I know the pain will eventually ease
By the time I feel the first summer breeze.

When Dusty enters the house again, he is surprised at how much time has passed. Lifting the fob watch, he winds it up, holding it to his ear to listen for signs of life. Its ticking mechanical heart beats out a rapid rhythm as the second hand races around obediently. He finds it funny how time moves slowly yet can also sprint away quickly.

When Alan had shown Dusty the watch years ago, he had said that it had belonged to a friend of the family. Alan had handled it like a precious artefact; something that was very important to him. Dusty had noticed this reverential care but did not think a great deal about it. That was to change on the day of Alan's funeral.

Alan's funeral was held on a sunny day. A PowerPoint summary set to music distilled Alan's life down to a series of images. In mumbled tones, people who had not seen each other for a lifetime shared the same space and related the usual mix of recollections and observations. Old conflicts and friendships were reignited in the emotionally-charged atmosphere.

Alan's sister, Emily, had spoken to Dusty about the watch and its origins. As her shaking hands held it out to him, she explained that the initials engraved on the back belonged to the person who had abused Alan as a child. She then related what her brother had told her.

His abuser had stolen so much time and quality of life from Alan that stealing the man's precious timepiece was the least Alan could do. It was a symbolic act of furtive defiance. He had urged her to live her life now and not let time slip away.

Standing in that chapel, her blue eyes freely sinking beneath watery pools, she looked at Dusty and implored him to live his life. 'It's what Alan would have wanted,' she said. 'Wind it up each day as a reminder to use all the time that you have to live well.'

He realised that it would be easy to just mark time and not strike out into the ocean of possibilities that curved beyond the horizon. With Emily's words echoing in his ears, Dusty became an island in a sea of people whose quiet chatter was white noise. He nursed a cup of tea that was beyond reviving and nodded to people in a manner that said: 'I acknowledge you, now please leave me alone.'

Calculating how long to stay in that place, he wandered back into the chapel which was halfway to where his car was parked. The pews were of a light-coloured timber and the walls were, for the most part, unadorned with anything suggestive of any denomination. Light glowed through windows that framed views of cultivated rose gardens. It was a pleasant enough space that projected a blandly reassuring aura. Placing his hand in his pocket to retrieve his car keys, his fingers felt the order of service. He had absently folded the paper so many times that it now felt like a failed origami experiment.

When he drove away, the one thing that remained lodged in his mind was the sight of Emily holding out the old fob watch for him to take. When their hands briefly touched, he felt her raw emotion surge through him. It was the moment when his empathy broke free of his self-absorption.

Safe harbour
Where the land curves around
An encircling hand, holding
Shallow water washing against fingers of rock
Exposed to the wind
Everything exposed to the chill
Boats moored, tethered in the bay
They turn in the wind
Always slowly turning
A man on the jetty leans into the wind
Rope over his shoulder
He pulls his tinnie across the water to the shore
Like it is a reluctant dog on a leash
This is a safe harbour
Where tethered boats keep changing direction
When I am not moving
Tethered in a safe harbour
The wind changes my direction
The way I am facing
Which way do I face?
When I power out of the safe harbour
Where should I go?

Dusty has taken himself out of the city to recharge his batteries. Each night he sleeps under canvas listening to the silence. Through the silence little sounds emerge. Maybe it is insect life; occasionally it may be something larger pawing the leaf litter. He burrows deeper into his sleeping bag, cocooned from the black night. In the morning his tent is covered in small flowers that have drifted off the trees in the night. He is surprised by the blossoms, but his campsite is close to the coast and there is just enough moisture in the air to maintain life.

Dusty lived a binary life, spending time in the city and the country. He loved both though he did prefer the country for the sense of connection it gave him to the natural world. Cities had become crowded with people who were disconnected from the environment and each other. But the county could also be a harsh and lonely place, especially with drought ravaging the land.

He is learning that empathy is not enough anymore. He would like to cultivate his empathy into compassion. Empathy for Dusty is feeling someone's pain or joy; compassion is acting on empathy and doing something to help. He can still see Emily on the day of the funeral. As that day recedes he realises that his desire to help others can sometimes be an unhealthy hunger to allow him to feel better about himself. To really help others involves listening skills—highly attuned listening skills. In the peace of the bush, he finds the space to slow down and listen to his heart.

A month passes, and Dusty is driving into Halls Gap in Victoria. This trip was planned, booked, and paid for before his commitment to Alan's ashes, a commitment he will fulfil in just two weeks. Dusty felt no compulsion to cancel this Grampians exploration; cliff top walks always had an irresistible magnetic attraction for him. He has wound the fob watch every day to remind himself to not waste his life. He is conscious of how much time and opportunity he has squandered over the years. He had never thought that Alan would die by suicide. He did not see it coming. He should have been noticing—and then understanding—his friend's distress. He lifts the watch to his ear and listens to the march of time as he looks heavenward. The sun has not yet risen, and stars still cover the sky.

In the dark, I can see
Easier in time. I let my
Eyes adjust to lack of light
By closing them to the reality
In my head then I am open to
The dark night. Halls Gap Victoria
Could not be darker, as mountains
Dam the light of coming day.
In that space, in that time
When I see a shape resolve
As something moves, a deer grazing
Becomes a roo. I am easily
Fooled in dark, it's easy to forget
I am fooled in the light
So very sure of what I can
Easily see, it's easy to forget
The need to close my eyes
To what I think I know
Then open them to dark mystery
The unique person in need who
Should know that I can close eyes
To my pattern of reality
So they feel safe enough to be
Seen as they really are
It is easier to see clearly
Closing eyes just for a moment
So my thinking comes after seeing
What is real, what love reveals.

The sun has burned away the last of the fog. Driving south from Halls Gap, he presses his foot down on the pedal and the car accelerates. He is just getting into the rhythm of driving at speed when he comes across a motor home lumbering along slowly in front of him. Unable to pass the huge vehicle, which has the aerodynamic features of a large brick, its size and shape block his view forward. When a large truck gradually fills his rear-view mirror, Dusty finds he is wedged between what is in front of him and what is behind.

In desperation, he pulls the car out over the centre line. A flock of sulphur-crested cockatoos would have been the only witnesses to the accident that didn't happen as Dusty hesitates in making the move that would have been a fatal one. The oncoming car blasts past him as he ducks back into his place in the queue. Yes, a queue is slowly forming behind him, but he is alive. The sudden rush of adrenaline in his bloodstream has made Dusty acutely aware of his surroundings. He transfers his imagination from inventive curses focused on the occupants of the motor home to pay more attention to what is around him.

He normally loves being on the open road with the horizon stretching out before him, but today he is distracted by another long journey that lies ahead of him. He plans to travel to Scotland for the purpose of spreading Alan's ashes from a mountain top; a task his friend had asked him to do years ago when they were young and healthy.

In their youth, Alan, Dusty, and a small group of friends had enjoyed mountain climbing and all manner of perilous activities with little thought to the consequences. That adventurous time ended for Alan and Dusty on the evening of the car crash, when Alan's legs were crushed. Living with constant pain for the rest of his life, he also lived with the knowledge that he could never climb another mountain. The resultant burns that branded Dusty's face and arms symbolised the guilt he felt every time he looked in the mirror.

He stops driving when he reaches Dunkeld. Mount Sturgeon sits like a lion at rest, framed by a bright yellow rapeseed field, yet this bright sight does nothing to change Dusty's dark mood. He dangles the fob watch from its gold chain and lets it spin like a coin on its axis. The story of how he got here whirls around in his mind as the grinding narrative rasps on his conscience one more time. The accident that changed Alan's life is recalled with clarity because Dusty was the one who had been behind the steering wheel on that dark, wet evening.

Relentless … solve one problem
Another one appears
Cry to God for help … help appears
Problem solved … mostly
Sometimes the problem isn't solved
But my perspective on the problem is changed
Why am I relentless in moving from one problem to another?
Why is it hard to slow down enough to give thanks?
Before the relentless accumulation of problems continues
Still, I am pursued by
God's love, God's grace, God's care
It does not seem to be rational
Who can understand it?
It is relentless.

The roadside lookout is a mere gash of dirt wide enough to park several vehicles. Dusty sits on the neglected picnic table to take in the view when a storm of dirt coats him from the truck that had been following behind as it blasts by. The cloud of dust takes its time to settle and from its midst, the motor home slowly appears. The lumbering vehicle is wrestled to a stop just five metres from where Dusty sits and the driver's door opens.

An elderly man slides out and places a step below the side door. The door opens and an elderly obese woman is carefully helped down to the ground. The man enters the vehicle and comes out again holding a small pug dog. He carries the bug-eyed creature to a tree, which the animal blesses with a steady flow that is uncomfortably audible in the absence of traffic noise. Dusty wished he could melt into the landscape and avoid eye contact with the people he had recently been cursing. When he looks up, the pug is staring at him with a pink-tongued manic smile that teeters between canine relief and vacuous lunacy.

The man approaches Dusty, greeting him with a cheery hello, and thanks him for his patience on the road. This was the last thing Dusty expected to hear from him. The old lady also approaches, and half an hour later they are still talking. Despite his initial desire to move on, Dusty finds himself drawn into the old couple's rambling conversation. He had expected condemnation from them, but the opposite has occurred.

Getting back on the road, he settles again into a steady driving pace. After passing through Warrnambool, he is well on his way to Apollo Bay when he realises he is beginning to enjoy the drive. As he thinks back to the old couple he met at Dunkeld, it becomes clear to him just how hard he has become on himself. Though he expects condemnation from other people, in fact, it rarely happens.

Viewing the sea and sky that looks so beautiful today, he nurtures a conviction to stay in this moment and notice the good things around him. He also decides to go gently on the car, on the day, and crucially, on himself.

Conviction before trial
Sounds backwards
But I am not in court
I am in life
Messy life
Where trials come
No one misses out
Trial and error, we all use it
If I have the conviction
To hold my moral compass
Between my head and my heart
Then my heart won't be hard on my head
And my head won't be hard on my heart
There is no condemnation
I am convicted before the trial
Convicted to use faith
Which is tried and tested
I try to be gentle on myself and not live in terror
For life is full of trial and error.

The next day is wet. Dusty is at Werribee because he made a mistake and turned off the highway too early. He wanders into a shed where a local group are restoring an old World War II plane—a B24 Liberator. He likes the name of the plane or at least the idea of something that liberates people.

Alan had never blamed Dusty for the accident that had shattered his legs when the car's tumbling descent was halted abruptly by a tree. For Dusty, looking at himself in a much harsher light than anyone else was a habit hard to shake.

Lost in his thoughts, Dusty is unaware of a pair of eyes watching him from the shadows, silent feet stalking him around the building. Moving outside, Dusty sits on an old bench protected from the weather by the eaves of the shed roof. It is here that it approaches him, black fur wafting in the breeze, its tail an extended question mark. Dusty extends his hand in a friendly gesture that is accepted. The cat sniffs him, rubs its face on his legs, and then rolls in the dirt.

It is often the little unexpected moments that Dusty treasures. Sitting with the friendly cat and listening to the rain hit the roof is something he will remember as especially serendipitous. The animal's curiosity and friendly interest make Dusty feel good. Of course, the feline may have just been attracted to the smell of his lunch. But it's never worth being too analytical about these special moments when they happen.

Glancing back through the shed's open doorway, Dusty wonders what it would have been like to fly in those warplanes. Admiration surfaces for the people who had fought those battles long ago. Both Alan and Dusty had fought their own battles for freedom over the years, but as he considers this he realises that there are two kinds of freedom worth fighting for; being free from something and being free to be something.

Freedom from and freedom to
Everyone wants to be free of something
But when they are free from something
They find out just how much
That something, bad as it was
Gave life structure, form, a pattern
Without that pattern, it's up to them
To follow the way, the truth into life
Life not defined by opposition to something bad
The freedom trap can be
To invent oppression where it does not exist
While missing those who are truly oppressed
Those not like us, it's often us and them
'I have come that they may have life'
And have it to the full
With the freedom to be
The only one that holds me back
Is me.

Back in Brisbane, Dusty's face is lit by the glow from his laptop. When not on the road his rediscovered enthusiasm to travel and explore new possibilities is manifest on his computer screen. Every search enquiry is related to travel. For so long, he has imprisoned himself in a kind of home detention. A self-imposed, self-limiting exile, though he had never thought about it that way. It had been an exile from the things that truly brought him life. While it had changed slightly in recent years, his travels were often centred on sourcing a specific type of wood for Alan. Now there was no need for such a venture.

Alan's request for Dusty to scatter his ashes from atop a mountain in Scotland seemed odd when they were young, but Alan had always been a little eccentric. Having lived the first twenty years of his life in Scotland, Alan had loved the country yet had removed himself from it, maybe because of its association with the place of his abuse. Alan's grandparents, many years ago, had been exiled from their home at Clydebank. The Clydebank Blitz was a Second World War horror story that Alan had related to Dusty as if it was a recent event, seeing as they both shared an interest in history and stories from yesteryear.

Then Alan's request came to the fore when Dusty had been allocated money from Alan's will to pay for this journey to Scotland. Alan had also left a letter which made it crystal clear which mountain his ashes should be spread from. It was less clear why this was important to Alan. Emily may have given Dusty a clue when she told him that he should move on to live his life. Was this whole exercise planned by Alan to get him out of the familiar and into the unknown?

Acknowledging that his eyes are tired from laptop use he switches off the device and his room is plunged into darkness. The trees outside seem to be applauding this moment, though Dusty knows that their leafy branches are actually moved by a dry wind that has been blowing all night. The breeze drifting in through the open window is laden with dust and smoke. Coughing, Dusty drinks some water from a bedside glass, letting the cool liquid soothe his parched throat. He has always had a thirst for doing the right thing and he is loyal to a fault. But like everyone, he is not without faults. Sacrificing oneself to help others sounds noble unless it becomes a self-punishing, self-limiting method of ameliorating guilt.

Looking back at any event in his past, he could pinpoint the moments that changed the outcome of his future. Hindsight, however, is not so beneficial when moving forward. If he had learned anything from his personal history, it was that no outcome was ever definite. Exiling himself to the safe and familiar, in a way limited the possible outcomes of his life story. History seemed to pivot on so many small moments that collectively moved things on, but the future always remained an undiscovered territory.

As Dusty sat in the dark room, he wondered how all his choices would play out across the broad scope of history. In short, did his actions really matter in the big scheme of things?

Time and tide
Ebb and flow
We live in
Big time but
We are here
A short time
The grand sweep of
Time and tide
Of big history
Washes all around
Sweeps us along
But all stories
All our stories
Ripen the history
Deepen the mystery
The mystery is
Our short time
Feeds big time
Every life matters
All are significant
Time and tide
Ebb and flow
Love and grace
In the eternal
Ocean of space.

Dusty has become a man on a mission, a man with a purpose. At first, birthed out of guilt, it was to learn more about his friend, Alan. Now, it has become a compulsion to transport his friend's ashes to their final resting place. The task of planning the trip helped him overcome the dark places in his thinking. Having something practical to focus on has given him strength.

His bag sits on his bed. He has repacked it several times, each time adding something else to combat the expected bleak Scottish weather. Does he have enough warm clothes? Looking through his wardrobe he notices how many clothes he no longer wears, and another purpose births in his mind. He removes unworn clothing from hangers and shelves. Then, wandering through the house, he collects more stuff he doesn't use anymore and forms a pile in the lounge room. Dusty keeps up with the news and he knows that the state of the economy is not good. He knows about the big issues of the day. He can see how global warming is changing everything. But every big issue wears a human face. There are people behind the statistics. Now more aware of the people in his neighbourhood, and their needs, he intends to donate the items for their use.

He returns to his bag. This time he reduces what he is taking to save on weight, which will aid him when hiking up and down hills. He also sheds any preconceived weight of expectation. The urn is nestled in the middle of his bag. The tin is on the floor. He considers taking it with him before sliding it under his bed. He is not sure why he hasn't opened it yet.

There is a tapping on the window, raindrops. The noise increases as the shower intensifies. There has been no rain for such a long time and the land is in drought. Dusty goes outside to the veranda and is bathed in the din of water hitting the corrugated roof. He soaks up the atmosphere and listens to the deluge. In ten minutes, it is all over. It was nice while it lasted.

He sits for a while watching the clouds retreat out to sea. Glancing down, he discovers another treasure trove of cluttered things worth donating. This launches him into an additional period of activity. It's funny how one thing leads to another. The sudden rain shower had led him outside and an hour later he has another pile of items. It really is much better for him now that he is less lost in his thoughts and more in the flow of everyday life.

I have found my place in the flow
Everyday life flows in to me
Some of it good, some of it bad
I have my place in the flow and it's not mine to control
When disturbing, unresolved things flow in and don't flow out
I go to the empty place I reserve for God to flow in
And life does flow in, in surprising diversity
It is surprising because it's not mine to control
It is not a place for answers, it's a place for life
It just comes, I just make a space and something comes
There are no words for it,
It's my experience of the eternal
I have my place in the flow
I may not control what flows in but I do have one choice
I will frame this choice as a question to myself
What kind of life flows out of me?

A week away from travelling overseas, Dusty is in the steady rhythm of work, rest, eat, and sleep, his days filled with activity. It is the regular rhythm familiar to everyone. On this Monday morning, he is driving to work when his car's heartbeat becomes irregular. The engine is still running but it sounds like it's ready to die. Dusty nurses the vehicle to a car repair workshop not too far away.

The mechanic makes a quick diagnosis. They can fix it if Dusty can hang around for a couple of hours. It's not what he would have planned for his day but Dusty is good at adapting to new circumstances. He sets out to explore an area he has never really noticed before, intentionally looking around and measuring his pace carefully.

The suburb has an eclectic mixture of old and new architecture. Old Queenslanders with broad verandas fail to compete with the height of new units that arise with increasing frequency as he approaches the train station. He plays a game of 'What would it be like to live here on this street?' and follows a walking path that cuts through a park and skirts along a creek that will eventually run into the sea.

A young man reclines on the grass in the sunshine, which has become quite hot. Dusty walks several metres past him, then he turns to look back. Something didn't seem right. The man lies stick straight as if he has been felled like a tree in a forest, and for some absurd reason, Dusty thinks of pictures he has seen of Hiroshima: the shadow images of people left on the ground after the bomb had dropped. Fear grips him. He hurriedly retraces his steps, drops to his knees and asks the obvious question, 'Are you ok?'

To Dusty's relief, the young man stirs and responds with slowly formed words that are delivered with a disturbing stammer. He says something about being hot and tired. A waft of alcohol gives evidence that the man has been drinking. Dusty offers him his water bottle which he accepts and drinks like he has been stranded in a desert.

Slowly at first, the young man tells Dusty he had walked a long distance to get away from home. When Dusty asks him where he was going he is casually told that he intended to throw himself off the bridge. The suicidal ideation seemed to leak out of the man. Dusty looks around seeking some trained professional to provide assistance, but they are alone in the park.

As the young man gradually becomes more focused in his speech, Dusty listens and offers neutral comments that fan the small flames of a conversation. He's eventually able to nudge the conversation around to what happens next. It is only when he is satisfied that the man is no longer a danger to himself that he leaves him. But even then, Dusty follows the man at a discreet distance to make sure that he does what he promised him. Watching the man enter a medical centre, Dusty would like to think that now he has the ability to offer wise words of counsel to anyone, but in practice, he finds the most effective strategy is to shut up and listen.

Looking for love in all the wrong places
Is the right thing to do
Everyone faces
Grief and loss
Trouble and pain
It's in these wrong places
That love does its work
It's the bitter that makes the sweet
Stand out in strong relief
Against the dark sky
The fingernail moon
A sliver of promise
Of repeating phases
The next that is different
Beckons with fear and excitement
We all live to die another day
To live another day and die another day
And with counterintuitive grace
And only partly by choice
And by the smallest of traces
Find love to go on
In all the wrong places.

Dusty walks back, noting that the houses that were new to him earlier now look very familiar. It's funny how a new place becomes normalised. His shirt clings to his damp skin. The day has turned humid and, on the dark western horizon, it looks like there may be a storm brewing. He collects his car and drives home.

Later that evening, a sudden crack of thunder shatters the air and his neighbourhood is plunged into darkness. Rather than search for a torch, Dusty goes outside and looks at the sky, lit periodically by incandescent flashes. Bolts branch out in all directions in a spectacular light show. When the clouds empty of rain and disappear, the stars reassert their presence. They are so much brighter without the shell of light pollution that normally domes around the city.

The lights come on again as power is restored, and Dusty is both relieved and a little sad, for the night sky had, for a little while, looked quite beautiful. He returns inside and finishes his day wondering what will happen to the young man he had met in the park.

He spends the next week at work, making up for the day he lost when his car broke down. He is employed by an outdoor adventure store located in the clutter of an inner-city suburb. He spends each workday selling people the means to escape into the wild. When the day of his departure to Scotland arrives, he gets up before sunrise in readiness for his early flight. A mild buzz of apprehension and nervous excitement had reduced his ability to sleep and he is already weary. Packed and ready to go, there is nothing left to do other than change his clothes, lock his front door, and stand outside under a sky that is still sprinkled with stars. His apprehension and compulsion to keep moving are soothed by the simple pleasure of watching the last of the night sky gradually surrender to the light.

Man of Dust
Walk this ground
Take some time
To look around
Pace yourself to my speed
I know your life
I know your need
Clear your mind
As you would clear this field
I send the rain
And truth revealed
Look up, not just down at the broken sod
The heavens declare the glory of God
Hear me in the silence
Hear me in the thunder
Walk this ground with childlike wonder.

It is during this quiet period that a flash of light crosses the sky.

A mote of dust becomes a burst of light
A slashed white line across the last of the night
A shooting star, in seconds, gone
But those seconds were bright in that time before dawn
So much of life passes over my head
But that's okay, I have my time and place
As this Man of Dust, this burst of life
I view your creation, in the morning cool
You bring me life, life to the full.

Another flash of light crosses Dusty's field of view. This time the source of light is terrestrial. The taxi approaches slowly, its hybrid engine quiet in the predawn darkness. After the peaceful beauty of the night sky, the low volume rap music that fills the car feels like a jarring intrusion to Dusty's heightened senses. It is a small mercy when the driver switches the radio off. The drive to the airport occurs in silence, as daunted by the long flight ahead of him, Dusty does not feel like conversing.

Once on the plane, Dusty settles in to read and watch movies while he travels east to west. He periodically checks the screen on the back of the seat in front of him, which displays an animation of his aircraft crossing a map of the world. He likes to be aware of his position in the world, but at such a high altitude he feels somehow divorced from the reality of his current location: somewhere in the sky, flying around the world to fulfil a promise made to his deceased friend.

Closing his eyes, he listens to the sound of the plane's engines and the regular drone lulls him into sleep. Thousands of feet up in the cold sky, encased in a steel tube thundering to its destination, Dusty dreams.

A fisherman's net, one of many, hand cast
By a cast of characters in the shallows
Stand, throw, haul, gently gather in
Sometimes they just stand.

They stand like the marker poles in the channel
Maybe they are speculating on the brief, white blossom
It should be light enough to spread in the air
But also weighted on the edges to crash down.

The fishers of men cast out love light enough
To open and expand in the air like a white blossom
Weighted down on the edges by their ability and experience
Love gently gathers in, gently hauls up from the depths.

Frustration at how far he can throw his net
Is tempered with the knowledge that the things
That weigh down and seem to limit love
Also help it to sink beneath the surface.

Beneath the surface, under water
In the drowning place looking up
From the depths where no hope lights the gloom
Beautiful blossoms expand like silent fireworks.

He wakes still tenuously connected to the strange dream. He is not sure if he was the one casting a net or if he was caught in a net. Odd dreams are not things he takes literally. He does, however, respond to how they make him feel. Right now, he feels quiet anxiety bubbling up from the depths of a great ocean of possibility. Many things are possible, but what will be the outcome of this trip? He makes a decision. When he has accomplished this task and returned home, he will open the tin containing items that Alan thought he should have.

He peers out the window, and while it is not visible through the heavy cloud, he knows that the sea lies far beneath him. It could be heaving in a fierce gale or mirror smooth. Dusty was born on a doomed boat somewhere down there in that vast emptiness. His parents died as the overloaded boat was smashed against a hidden reef, leaving him to the tender mercy of a well-intentioned foster family. His name is not his own, he doesn't even know what his birth name is, or even if there was time to be given one. 'You make a name for yourself as you grow into this world' someone had once told him. Growing up, his name was known to the police but Dusty never graduated to a life of crime. His own story seems improbable even to him, but he is here now, living proof that dreams can come true. His parents dreamed of a better life for him. He feels sad that they never got to fulfil their own dreams.

The hours move slowly now as the aircraft passes over multiple arbitrary borders that delineate people from each other. Dusty feels no connection with his parents' native country. Vietnam is as foreign to him as it was to his foster family. Having been born on the ocean, he sometimes regards himself as a citizen of the world. His facial features suggest that his biological parents came from different countries but that is a mystery he will never solve. Dusty lives in and for the moment; at least that is his intention. His loyalties lie with people not abstract concepts like nationality and culture. He settles in to try to get some more sleep as the plane gradually approaches its destination.

George Johnston

A thin veneer floats on a salty ocean
Covering lies and half-truths, myths, and misconceptions
Conceived and gestated in fear-soaked
Black and white, us and them narratives
The fresh water of subversive love seeks out the fault lines
Where people often seek fault in others
While missing the truth in themselves
Love soaks through the surface of life
Submersive love calls me to go beneath the surface
To the heart of things where head knowledge works
In concert with the heart of me, the part of me that knows
That words are not enough
And I should save my breath, maybe hold my breath and go
Beneath the surface
Where God's immersive love is all
Where words don't just sink into my head
Where I sink submissive into God's subversive love.

Dusty arrives in Edinburgh, sleepwalking into a new land, a new day. What day is it? Today. That will do; it is today. He trusts that his phone will recognise the time zone when it's fired up again. It does. There are crowds of people compressed in the cavernous space of the airport. Security is high. He goes with the flow and is filtered through a series of checkpoints, flashing his passport, the document that categorises his identity. He smiles at the border security officials and answers their questions, aware they have him pegged as being of interest—and not just because the burns on his face make his smile awkward. He may believe that he is a citizen of the world, but the world is divided, and his ethnicity is always given special attention.

He passes through these tense moments and is at last on the street in his rented car. Here, on the other side of the world, everything is different, and everything is the same; much like most cities around the world. They all have different flavours, but the same type of fear pervades the streets. Fear of the other, the stranger, and the ones who don't fit in. Yet everyone must fit into some category, how else can they know what to sell you?

He leaves the city with its clutter of advertising signs and relaxes as the urban landscape gives way to green hillsides. It has been a long journey and he is so relieved to see open space again that he makes several stops from driving to enjoy each view and stretch his legs. Fatigue from his journey does not dampen Dusty's appreciation of Loch Lomond when he finally arrives at Balmaha. Sitting in his parked car he removes the fob watch from his pocket and winds it up. Listening to its small mechanical heartbeat and remembering his commitment to make the best of each moment, something catches his attention.

The loch contains a perfect reflection of the hillsides. A small boat lies discarded on the pebbly shore. He exits the car and photographs it, all the time trying to capture some essence of this moment. The boat he was born on is long gone, but sometimes he speculates on the people who made that journey. He owes them a great debt, for their sacrifice allowed him to grow up in a relatively safe country. He is not far from his accommodation for the night—an easy walk—yet he doesn't immediately move off. Sleep wants to shut down his senses but he is entranced by the view. It is obvious to him that this moment is a time to rest and be thankful.

Discarded on the loch
It lies grounded on the
Earth where it was made
It does not belong here
It lies where it should
Float free and I can
Only speculate on what
Happened long ago
It is a pale reflection
Of what it was
Or might have been
Did it carry people
Like me across the water?
What did those people carry
With them across the water?
Their hopes and dreams
Gone like the love that
Made this boat then
Discarded it on the loch
It is now grounded on the
Earth where it was laid to rest
I now rest with it
Alive to the stories it invokes
I capture an image
This peaceful image
Of time and tide
A reminder that things discarded
Can still add balance and beauty
Charm and character
Grounded on the muddy earth
I captured an image
That I will retain in memory
And not leave
Discarded on the loch.

Dusty treads the main road in Balmaha. Many solid stone buildings line the narrow footpaths, on both sides, yet it is mostly quiet. Dusty had heard so much about this place from Alan that it already existed in his mind long before he arrived. Still, he is in a state of transition, waiting to be more grounded in the reality that is all around him. Stretching stiff neck muscles, his eyes are drawn to an old cottage bearing a sign that indicates he has reached his accommodation. Like many of the village structures, its thick stone exterior is drab, as if the outside world has worn down any desire for frivolous external decoration. Though unseemly, he knows the cottage offers insulation from the harsh, cold weather, and inside he will find the provision of warmth and protection from the elements.

Entering his small, cosy room, Dusty opens his bag and removes several items. Unfolding a handful of documents, he indulges in his love of maps. He is here primarily to spread Alan's ashes, but he will also take Emily's advice and walk several mountains. As he studies the maps, one location stands out—a place he will not visit on this trip. It is in the confines of the city; an old church, the old church where Alan had suffered so much in his early years. He knows that some people find sanctuary within such a building, but he supposes it's dependent on the history they have with the place.

Dusty suddenly remembers some photographs Alan had obtained of the interior of the church, and it is only just now that Dusty makes a connection. The old photographs were of the intricately carved wood that lined the interior of the building. When Alan whittled his creations, was he going back to that time in his life? Did he actually draw inspiration from the place?

The windowpane shudders as the howling wind assaults the cottage. Dusty looks out but can only see his reflection peering back at him from the gloom. It will likely be the same when he ventures out tomorrow. The more he pushes out into the natural world, the more he must rely on his storehouse of inner resources to deal with whatever he encounters. He knows that he could try to insulate himself from the harsh realities of life, but they will still shape him with or without his acceptance.

Tomorrow, he will stand on a geological fault line at a place called Conic Hill. But right now, Dusty is standing on a fault line between his past and future. His history is not like Alan's, living within the insulating walls of church or family. Dusty feels nurtured by harsh, beautiful landscapes and has been a bit of a loner for several years, but that reality appears to be gradually crumbling.

George Johnston

Ice cold like a blast from the past
The wind makes my eyes cry, my hands numb
The cloud ceiling opens up as sun lights
Bluebell woods and yellow gorse
Gone from the boxes people live in
The city is a child's model town laid out
Glasgow barely visible
Beyond its boundaries, mountains
The sight that shouts out a story
Of rugged contours that rise and fall
The people shaped
By the land with or without
Their knowledge or consent
Conic Hill sits on a fault line
Fault lines shape the land
And mock our desire
To live in neatly ordered boxes
Life thrives outside neatly ordered modernity
Where, from the top of a mountain
You see another and another
On and on as the past and future
Bracket the present
Spend lots of time out here
And your hands may be cold
But your heart won't be numb
To the big tangled landscape
And your place
In its story.

Conic Hill was a good warm-up for Dusty. He will walk higher tomorrow when he tackles Ben Lomond, then the day after he will tackle Ben Donich. Alan had been quite specific in his instructions, stressing that his ashes be spread from its peak. Why Ben Donich? Dusty wasn't sure; there was a lot about his friend that he didn't know. After the car accident, Alan had retreated to the confines of a cluttered shed. But within that shed, Alan had spent hours carving out a new life for himself. It just wasn't the kind of life he had originally planned. It also wasn't the kind of life that appealed to Dusty. So, he assumed that Alan's seclusion was due to long-term depression. Yet what had Dusty done to help his friend? Not enough; it felt like he had not done enough.

Time and circumstance had loosened the bond of friendship between them. Looking back, it was easy for Dusty to interpret all that he knew of Alan's life in the light of how it ended. He saw evidence everywhere, little clues that he had missed about Alan that seemed to lead to one inevitable outcome, his death by suicide. He knew that this hypothesis was filtered through his knowledge of Alan's suicide and magnified by his feelings of guilt. But if he romanticised Alan's life through rose-coloured glasses totally ignoring how he died, as some had done at the funeral, then that story also was incomplete. If he summarised Alan's life as one inevitable slide to doom, then he too ignored that Alan had what we all have: the greatest gift of life—choice.

Dusty could have walked up Ben Donich earlier in his trip, but he had chosen to wait until he had acclimatised, and also for a better weather window. Once again, he unfolds his map. The route for his walk up Ben Lomond has been calculated, though, if needed, he is prepared to alter his plans if the weather turns foul. He may even decide to change tack on a whim once he sets out. In the past, he has found great joy in disregarding boundaries drawn on maps and relished the freedom of his own explorations. The biggest boundaries for Dusty have been the ones that have had him thinking that there were only limited choices on offer. He has had enough of that. His resolution to fully live his life is growing along with his desire to write his own story and not be bound by a passivity ordained by some predetermined script. Life is a mixture of good and bad and from this mix comes a richness that is beautiful.

His bag is packed for a range of weather conditions—bad and good—and he goes to sleep amidst a buzz of apprehension and excitement. Tomorrow is another day waiting to be discovered and explored.

Ben Lomond
Walking all day
Through snow falling
Then quickly melting up
Cold air roiling round and round
We move up and up and up and spy
Cloud forests in the sky seeded further ahead
They coil down Loch Lomond over islands over glens
This mountain is the beacon hill in times gone
Marking boundary lines between people
Beacon fires may have been lit here but
Now as it always did, it marks the line
Where water flows east or west
Feeling the size of the mountain
In every step, in every false summit
We have nothing but praise for we see
The effort spent, the something gained
Legs and shoulders may be pained
But beacon fire warms our hearts
As—small upon the peak—we find that which we seek
No boundaries just God's adventure playground
Mountains as far as you can see
Carved by water from those cloud forests in the sky
And sealed with love from their creator
A love that will not die.

He savours the fresh taste of the cold air. Having reduced his internet use for the duration of this trip he now has a voracious appetite for the world around him that can't be satisfied by his daily news feed. He had forgotten how much the blue-sky silence could satisfy his need for a quiet cleared space. In this space, without the distraction of a constant flow of information, he is more connected with himself. It is life unplugged; an acoustic oasis devoid of electrical amplification.

As Ben Lomond is a popular destination, he has had his fair share of company. For the most part, his fellow walkers were a very friendly bunch. A few were unprepared and they strained up the mountain with beetroot-red faces due to hearts struggling to pump blood to where it was needed. At least they were here, in the clouds on the mountain. If they were to die here at least they would have lived.

He has a theory that many people die before their death because they don't know how to live while they are alive. Dusty had no desire to tell people how to live but he would encourage people to find what brings them life and be bold enough to share some of that life with others. He noticed how much modern life, with all its distractions, seemed to dull genuine connections between people.

The variable wild weather challenges everyone on the mountain. Within a short space of time, the sun gives way to wind, then rain, then snow, then clear, then hail, and then clear again. Several times on the way up, Dusty questions the wisdom of his actions but he presses on. He can see the top and it draws him onward and upward. When he finally reaches it, the reward at the top is a sense of achievement that brings deep satisfaction. When the clouds part, the drama of the moment is not lost on the people who have assembled on the summit. Everyone enjoys the beautiful view that is revealed.

The crowd standing with him have all climbed the same mountain, on the same day, with the same weather, but looking around at the diverse group, he can see that different obstacles would have challenged each person. Not everyone who started out has made it to the top and that was okay. There was always another day and maybe another challenge more suited to them. But those who have pressed on, and overcome their difficulties, are now enjoying the simple pleasure of the view laid out before them.

For all their beauty, the mountains of Scotland are relatively devoid of trees. But the barren harshness resonates with Dusty and he enjoys observing the panorama. It's like he is standing on a giant map, a satellite view more detailed than anything on the internet. This is real life up close and personal but high enough to see things in a clearer fuller perspective. A part of him would like to help other people climb these mountains, just so they could see what he is seeing now.

George Johnston

From the top
Toy cars driven
By model citizens
Move on roads
That line the glens
Deep between
An endless sweep
Of peaks that
Rise and fall
And rise and fall
With only some
Places where
People driven to
Drive can go
On roads
That line the glens.

From the top
Cloud shadows
Sail across the mounts
With shapes
That ever change
A moving picture
Painted on a canvas
That is never flat
On the panting path
To where this painted
Moving picture perplexes
With perspective shifts

We survey this place
Where people
Are driven to walk
On paths
That line the Bens.

From the top
Small hilltops
Are the tops
Of mountains
With toy people
On the skyline of
Ridged silhouettes
They inch across our
Line of sight
Sighted through
The lenses of
Binoculars held
With hands blasted numb
By the ice winds
That must be blowing on
These matchstick people
As like us they seek
Balance and are driven like us to
The tracks that line the sky.

From the top
Small victories
Join together as we scramble

Over rocks
With nothing ever
Level or smooth
Every sliding step
A step away from
A trip but the whole trip
Is worth every step
For we have already fallen
For the view from the top
Where so many little things
Set against that big sweep
Of endless mountains
All join together
To make a whole
To make us whole
We hold the view somewhere
Inside forever this
View from the top.

From the bottom
From the depths
From the dark
From the gloom
There is a choice
There is a way
There is a hope
To choose your hill
To choose your climb
To choose your summit

Which can be reached
Which can be seen
Which can be felt
If you seek
You will find
There is no need
To feel left behind
Joined together
We can scramble
And help you when we can
But it will be
Your journey
Your track
Your view
From the top.

The day he will carry Alan's ashes one last time begins under a clear sky. Dusty leaves his car on a road just off a mountain pass called Rest and Be Thankful. He likes the name. He sees an old military road that the signage says was completed in 1750. The old road seems stable while the new road further up the slope looks to be under repair from a landslide which is quite frequent in these parts.

Aware of the challenging terrain and the false summits that can induce feelings of dashed hope in climbers, he urges himself onwards. Only occasionally does he look back at the safety of the mountain pass he is leaving behind. When he reaches the true pinnacle, he rests and most definitely is thankful as the clarity of the view from this point is amazing. He can see the distant islands of Arran and Ailsa Craig way beyond the Firth of Clyde and the mainland.

There is also a sense of clarity for Dusty; all that is distant in time and space, while not any closer, feels more connected. Dusty has a habit of remembering what he should have forgotten and forgetting what he should have remembered. Yet in this moment of lucidity, he is fully present to the sadness and the beauty encompassing him. Positive and negative emotions no longer battle within. Aware of both, he is at peace with both; he feels more balanced.

He removes the urn from his backpack and is about to spread Alan's ashes when he notices three sheep watching him. They seem to be everywhere in Scotland. Like a little crowd of witnesses, they stand with him on the summit, their presence giving him the strength he needs. He moves a few short metres from the sheltered side of the peak to where the cold wind howls across the top and opens the urn. Before he's even released the breath he's holding, the wind scours the ashes out. A fine cloud of ash puffs into the sky, an insubstantial sight when viewed against the grandeur of the landscape.

The sheep have gone back to eating grass and Dusty returns to the sheltered side of the summit out of the wind. Peace permeates him. It is the peace of having completed something important—fulfilling Alan's wishes. He does not rush down the mountain.

Two months pass. The world turns. Dusty has turned over a new leaf in his story and is back in Brisbane where he now sits in his kitchen. He has just got over the effects of jet lag and is regarding Alan's sealed tin through bleary eyes. About to open it, he hears movement outside on the footpath; the rattle of wheels. Peering out through his narrow window on the world, he expects to see the lady with the pram trundling past, but it is not her. Another person he has not seen before is walking by pushing a shopping trolley. On impulse, he goes outside on the pretence of pulling out some weeds—a task he seldom does—and greets good morning to the stranger. To his surprise, they strike up a conversation.

A gentle man and a scholar
Polite and measured in his words
Positive with a small smile
He chats of knowledge, experience, wisdom
He is so easy to like, such a gentle soul
He does not push his own agenda
Instead, he pushes a shopping trolley
His life in a battered suitcase.

He tells of his life
As a nomad following the seasons
But crops are failing and some farmers die
By their own hand and the others may find it easier
To pay a backpacker who does not get super.

This man is not bitter
Maybe it's his age
An age of reason from following the seasons.

In the city there are
More people, more help, more risk
In the country there are
Fewer people, less help, less hope.

What hope have I got to give him?
He did not ask for hope
He did not really ask for anything
But was very grateful for what he had
And he loved to chat and I loved to listen.

I did not meet a problem
A symptom of an unhealthy cruel world
I met a man of knowledge, experience, wisdom
Polite and measured in his words
A gentleman and a scholar.

Dusty has enjoyed chatting with this gentleman and watches, with a smile on his face, as he pushes the trolley down the footpath. Expensive high-performance cars crawl along the congested road. Most drivers cocooned within their vehicles can't help but notice the man with a trolley. Their passengers, however, don't turn their eyes away from their video screens. They have movies on the move. It's like people are outsourcing their imagination to Hollywood or Bollywood or some other place; any other place than the one they are travelling through. Moving closer to the kerb, Dusty noticed that one of the cars has two news channels playing on a split-screen. The passenger sitting in front of the screen also has their neck bent over a portable device. With so many possible distractions, it is not surprising that many drivers only give the man with the trolley a cursory glance. Trolley man stops to dig through a rubbish bin looking for something vaguely nutritious.

Dusty sets his mind on opening the sealed tin tonight after dinner. He has been speculating on its contents. Maybe it contains a journal with some grand revelations regarding Alan. As he walks back through the creaking gate to his house, he wonders why some people end up cosseted inside expensive cars and others scavenge scraps on the street. Why are our stories so different? What makes that difference—chance, fate, circumstance, luck?

Dusty never drank to excess, but on the night of their accident, his alcohol consumption was way over the limit. He never drank again after that night. Alan had never drunk much before the accident but afterwards, he became an alcoholic just like his parents. It was like the consequences of the accident had tipped Alan over the edge into a coping mechanism that he had seen modelled by his parents. When he had eventually eased off on the drinking and taken up carving, Dusty had felt that his friend was only swapping one obsession for another.

As he prepares dinner, searching his pantry for ingredients he notices something at the back of a high shelf. It is a bottle of double malt whisky, once a favourite of his. He had forgotten about it. He picks it up and places it on the table, eyeing it salaciously and wondering if he could be tempted to get on the booze and slide down that slippery slope. The fact that he is having this thought negates the probability of it happening. His evening meal is flavoured with chilli and consumed with an undercurrent of unease. The whisky bottle, like Alan's tin, remains untouched for another night.

I have seen him go
From the top of the tree
Then back to his roots
To charge off full throttle
Then end off a bottle
Or two or three
Or four or more
And I wonder why
We are different
Different addictions
Everyone has them
To some degree though
Not always harmful
Go and see him
Because it could be you
One day at the bottom
Of some bottle though
Your addiction
May not be drink
You would be wrong
If you think you couldn't
Tip over the edge
By some twist of
fate or chance or design
Stay drunk on the life
That helps you walk straight
In the spirit that's true
And stay connected
With ears to listen
And a heart
That knows what to do.

The morning sun illuminates the unopened bottle on Dusty's kitchen table; its amber hue is the first thing that he noticed when he entered to make breakfast. Alan's older relatives had called whisky the 'water of life'. He smiles when he thinks of an old gentleman he once worked with who would have a hot toddy every night and lecture everyone on the health benefits of regular shots of whisky. Always sceptical when one thing was elevated as the sole answer to good health, Dusty accepted the old mantra about moderation. Though lately, he had come to realise that life could not always be effectively summed up in a cliché. What brings life to someone could destroy life in others.

He is still half asleep when he turns the radio on, filling the kitchen with sounds of an old song. As he looks out on the world through tired bleary eyes, 'I can see clearly now the rain has gone' reverberates around the room. Would it be a 'bright sunshiny day' today? What did that even mean? On the horizon, a burnt orange glow promised much but it wasn't the sun that was needed, it was more rain.

He switches on the kettle to make a cup of tea. It is an old kettle that splutters and wheezes like a steam train climbing a steep hill. The steam rises to the high shelf enveloping Alan's carvings which seem to indignantly glare down at Dusty.

When the noisy kettle finally stops, Cher begins belting out 'If I could turn back time…' Hitting the switch on the radio, he lets the silence in again. If Dusty could have his time again, he would correct his mistakes. He would avoid driving the car on that night and Alan would be uninjured and still alive. But then Dusty would have had no reason to give up his drinking. Could he have become an alcoholic, in time, but for the accident? How would his life have turned out then?

He sits in his living room. Not much living happens in this room. The slim television is connected to multiple streaming services, but it is currently just a blank screen. It is a window on the world that he often starts his day with. But not today. This morning he will finally open the tin.

Living the dream
Sleepwalking through
Someone else's stories
Fed by a diet of movies
And games and music
And someone else's
Narratives written for
Consumption and profit
Following scripts written
For us so that we can
Dream and live on
The food for thought
That has already been
Predigested and spat out
As fresh and new but
What is new under the sun?
When every story
When every verse
Is dreamed up by those
Who live in a past that only happened
For them
Or a future that could only ever be
Theirs and theirs alone
For alone we come into the Storyverse
And alone we leave
And whatever we have
And whatever we fight
Should be just our dream
Our story to write.

Dusty uses a knife to slice through the sticky tape ringing the tin's lid. With the seal broken, he can pry the lid off. For a moment, he feels like Howard Carter breaking into Tutankhamen's tomb. The sight of the Scottish terriers smiling up at him from what was originally a shortbread tin instantly dissolves this ludicrous thought.

The contents surprise him. There are photographs, school reports, sporting medals, old coins from different countries; a schoolboy's treasures. There are also old medical reports and correspondence, which he ignores. Alan had received years of treatment after the accident. It is in Dusty's nature to be a little squeamish about medical things, so he sweeps those aged papers into the bin.

There are also index cards titled by names he does not recognise. These interest Dusty more than the dull medical papers. The cards seem to contain short biographies. Who were these people? When he turns the cards over, he notices that each one has a sketch of a different carved figure. Dusty is confused. Had Alan named his little figures and kept details on each one?

The notes detailed the type of wood to be used, the types of knives needed, a planned schedule for working on the creation, and a profile for each little figure. Dusty saw with new eyes just how much discipline, patience, and dexterity was required to carve life into the little figures.

Dusty hesitates a moment when he discovers a dog-eared journal. Gingerly opening it, time passes without notice as he becomes lost in the written monologue of his old friend's life. At first, the contents seem to be a disjointed collection of thoughts and recollections, and then a pattern emerges. Each section of the narrative is a puzzle piece that brings clarity to the image of Alan that Dusty has in his mind. At times he senses his old friend speaking to him directly.

Some of the writing refers to the photos that have spilt out of the tin. Sorting through the pictures, he can place them in context to the text Alan has written and sees how the photos represent the times and places Alan has chosen to preserve. It was his life, his story. Though Dusty can't fully understand all of it because it is not his lived experience he is glad that Alan owned the story and felt the need to write it down.

There are several poems in the tin, but one catches Dusty's attention more than the others. Easily imagining Alan speaking the words he reads and listens intently.

Into the Storyverse,
My story spreads in
Concentric circles
Like ripples in water
Or soundwaves
In an echo chamber.

Lost in transmission
Flawed perception
Sinks my story
Like a pebble dropped
Through ocean depths.

Random circumstance
Or predestined events
Have taken me
Over the horizon
Where previous
Terrible chapters
Read like they are
Someone else's story,
But memory recalled
Is memory reconstructed
In the context of today.

Today I live with
Disconnected stories
Food for thought
Reduced to snack-sized
Soundbites
People offer the
Hope and encouragement
They found on Facebook
Nothing can replace
The lived experience
Of the Storyverse.

Closing Alan's journal, Dusty leans over to lace up his boots. It is time to move on. It is time to move out into a new day. He remembers occasions when Alan had spoken about the Storyverse. At the time it was an abstract concept to Dusty. 'No one should live their own story in isolation,' Alan once told him. Dusty has trouble reconciling Alan's words with his actions. But words state intention and everyone stumbles their way through life in a meandering path of quiet desperation. He knows it isn't always obvious when someone is struggling because everyone experiences and expresses life differently.

He looks around his house at the artefacts he has collected over time; an eclectic collection of items he cannot throw out. Shells from the coast, empty bottles, Alan's carved figures. To anyone other than Dusty they would be just a collection of junk. Yet for him, each one tells a story. But they are easily forgotten, easily lost to memory. So Dusty resolves to tell himself his own story from the beginning; to begin rewriting and reframing his life from a gentler perspective.

Dusty does not think of himself as a good man but he has a devotion to people that transcends his mistakes. He is driven on by love even if he does not articulate it clearly. 'Let my actions speak before my words.' He verbalises this and feels foolish as there is no one to hear it. The feeling drains away and he resolves to be kind to himself.

On the way out the door, he realises he has misplaced his keys. A flush of heat runs through him and he is about to berate himself, then he captures the thought before it captures him. Go gently. He retraces his steps and finds the keys on the shelf, sitting on an old book he had forgotten about. Pocketing the keys, he brushes the dust off the book cover and opens it. The book contains a whole series of places and things he had listed years ago. It is a book that holds the naive aspirations of a much younger man.

Putting it down, he opens the front door and walks out through his overgrown garden to the street. There is a momentum building inside him. It is a determination to not try to resolve everything but to just keep moving into the new. He will live his own authentic story and listen carefully to everyone he meets. He steps into the light of this new day. He has new mountains to climb and new people to meet along the way.

Upward mobility carries me forward
By this, I mean my tired body
I am not a social climber, I climb up
By choice, becoming a dot on the landscape
The horizon is wide and uncluttered by modernity
The land is timeless, vast, and empty, yet
It teems with life, that flies or crawls or hops or runs
I must fit into its rhythms, be that hot or cold
Wet or dry, often all of these things in one day
Adapt and find the comfortable pace to keep moving
Comfort is a different concept as the hours and kilometres flow by
I am part of a bigger picture, that make my
Small time concerns less relevant, less pressing
There are endless obstacles so I have to look down to my feet
Out of necessity, I take the practical steps to move
Looking down to move up
Trying not to fall over at any pace
I am falling upward into grace
Its downward mobility carries me forward.

A week, a month, and then years go by. Dusty embarks on several journeys that expose him to a diversity of life experiences. He becomes a chronicler of stories, often gathering them from those on the margins of society. He breathes life into their stories. The process breathes life into Dusty. Sometimes he writes people's stories; sometimes he helps them to find their voice. Wherever he goes he takes with him the knowledge that everyone's story matters.

His travels seem random but there is a method in his madness. He always interrupts his journey when he senses a need. Listening with quiet compassion, he reflects on what he hears with concise coherency. People respond to his gentle acceptance and see him as wise. But for Dusty, the wisdom he took a lifetime to learn can't be taught; it can only be experienced. He has seen so many who try to help people go straight to the solution before understanding the problem.

As an elderly man, he moves slower than when younger, but he is still moving; still driven by a desire to explore and discover. As his body ages, his heart and mind have returned to the simplicity of childlike wonder. In this second half of life, there is no striving to achieve or measure up. He spends less time posting opinions online and more time being a safe listening post for anyone.

He returns to the Tasmanian beach where forty years ago he had seen the land burn, his mind weighed down by stories that have accumulated like the sediment on the sand bar on which he now stands. He walks out onto the sand that juts with futile defiance into the sea.

As he walks along this narrowing piece of land, he knows that by anyone's definition he is now ancient. Does anyone want to hear the tales gathered by an old man? He longs to have these stories published, printed, distributed. In his mind, he is a relay runner eager to pass on a baton to the next runner. In reality, he now shuffles to the finish line with no crowd to cheer him on. At least none that he can see.

There is no one around to hear the soft patter of his bare feet on the sand. Where there is life, there is hope, and an ocean of possibility still calls him to float freely into its embrace. He enters the water and looks over his shoulder at the beach, thinking that his backpack looks like a small cairn. It contains a tin where he has stashed his stories.

It is a beautiful moment when the salty sea supports his tired body. He floats in the still ocean staring up at the eternal sky. Dusty feels suspended in time and at peace with himself. He leaves the Storyverse; natural causes sinking him like a stone into someone else's memory; someone unconnected with all of this; someone new.

Later that evening, their curious hands will open his old backpack as ripples spread across the Storyverse.